THE LABYRINTH OF ROOMS:
AN ARCHITECTURAL ALLEGORY

Ali AlYousefi

T0283780

ORO
EDITIONS

CONTENTS

to my mother

ACKNOWLEDGMENTS

I want to thank my friends Dalia E. Aly, Scott Deisher, Noor Al-Fayez, Miranda Mote, and Samos for their helpful advice and constant encouragement.

I also want to thank Dalal Musaed AlSayer, Hamed Bukhamseen, Franca Trubiano, and David Leatherbarrow for talking to me about how Word documents become books.

I also want to thank Sharaf Studio for actually turning my Word document into the book you are holding.

I also want to thank Gordon Goff for taking interest in my book idea, Kirby Anderson for guiding me through the publishing process, and Kate Kinast for copyediting the manuscript.

I also want to thank John McMorrough for contributing the foreword that so perfectly starts the book.

This book came out of an interest in pixel art that started when I participated in the SADI 2022 artist residency, organized by Sadu House, Kuwait. To them, I am grateful.

On Perusing Ali AlYousefi's "Machines for Asking Beautiful Questions"

What do we know, and how do we know it? Must knowledge necessarily be gained from personal experience, or can it be gleaned from disembodied representations? Or, for that matter, is representation simply considered a form of mediated experience? Such questions are the epistemological concerns throughout Ali AlYousefi's *The Labyrinth of Rooms: An Architectural Allegory*. At first glance, it is a simple story, someone trying to understand (and escape) the riddle of spaces and sequences in which they unexpectedly find themselves. While the elucidation of these imbroglios is for each reader to derive for themselves, a few preparatory notes on the means and methods of this work are in order, as orientation for the passages to follow.

First, regarding the setting: at least in Greek mythology, the original labyrinth was designed by Daedalus (alternately referred to as an architect or an artificer), constructed to contain the monstrous Minotaur. When Theseus comes to slay the beast, it is only with instruction from Daedalus himself that he can find his way into the structure ("go forwards, always down, and never left or right"), and only by following a golden thread which he unfurled over the course of his entrance is Theseus able to find his way back out. This structure and others like it have been alternately called a labyrinth or a maze, and though now used interchangeably, the terms have distinct connotations.

The maze, originating in Middle English, is a shortened form of *amaze* (denoting delirium or delusion) and implies a bewildering multiplicity of directions and paths (one can get lost in a maze). On the other hand, labyrinth derives from the Greek *labúrinthos* and initially describes any complex underground structure; however, over time, it has become associated with a single path proceeding teleologically to a center, albeit with twists and turns (a labyrinth is a path in which the journey is one of discovery). The maze is associated with uncertainty (as in "a maze of confusion"), and the labyrinth with meditation (a prayer path, for example). The golden thread of AlYousefi's labyrinth is its form (decisively a labyrinth with progress through it relatively assured), but this trajectory is reinforced and complicated by its description of image and word. As an architect and a writer (the intersection of the two is more significant than one would initially imagine, as both are concerned with the arrangement of shapes and significances), AlYousefi's renderings of phrase and figure offer aligned, but not entirely congruent, delineations.

This labyrinth is presented as a series of rooms (as noted in the title), each expressed in a single image, portrayed in a rudimentary, pixel-like, fashion, occupying a 15 x 15 grid with no detail other than the articulation of solid and void (which is assumed to be wall and space). The effect of these low-resolution

(15 x 15 = 225) delineations as images is that their
legibility oscillates between architectural typologies
(corridors and alcoves, ziggurats and hypostyle halls),
shapes (flowers and snakes, gears and circuit boards),
and QR codes (the matrix barcodes, which when
read with the appropriate device provide identifiers,
locators, and routing data). In addition to these
proliferate associations, if one understands these
figures according to the architectural convention
of a "plan" (a drawing as a horizontal cut through
a structure) they take on a unique performance.
In this case the plan is apprehended not only by its
gestalt (its overall legibility) but by a tracing of the
labyrinth's path with the eye, which draws the reader
into a particular form of inhabitation. A series of
perspectival views, which are typically understood as
the most immersive drawing convention, might seem
a better representational choice to hold the reader
enthralled, as a plan's general purpose is to understand
a structure's overall and abstract organization; however,
deciphering the route through the labyrinth offers
a haptic form of immersion. In tracing the imagined
path of the narrator, the reader in turn experiences
the labyrinth for themselves.

      The description of spaces also extends from
the visual into the textual. The discriminations of the
forms encountered are described in a series of texts
whose formats range from expositional to expressive –

alternately declarative, poetic, and existential.
The text associated with each plan-image is written
in third person narration which, in its descriptive clarity
of the physical and the psychic, puts the reader
into the viewpoint of the amnestic protagonist. These
descriptions are not specifically addressed to the
reader, but rather are matter-of-fact descriptions
of the running tally of the spaces encountered by
the story's subject (whose only descriptor is that of
"Human") and along with it, an associated rumination
on their significance (both of the spaces and of the
subject). With these externalized internal monologues,
the narrator/writer shares their questions with the
audience/reader and informs their own imagination
of what is transpiring – an act of collaboration, where
the product of writing informs, but does not dictate,
the products of reading.

　　　Dislocated, disoriented, and discombobulated.
In this story, as in life, we start where we start, grasping
to make sense of where we are and where we are going.
AlYousefi's *The Labyrinth of Rooms* sits within the
sub-genre of architectural narratives of disorientation
and discovery, which, from Plato's "Parable of the Cave"
to J. G. Ballard's "Report from an Unidentified Space
Station," offer tales of deciphering, orientation, and
progression (locating of the self, transposition of the
self by orientation, the setting off in a new direction).
Each room, each image, each text, and each page

is a parable. As these stories unfold, the interplay of images (literal and mental) and narratives (external and internal) reveals an expanding constellation of meanings, an aesthetic dimension which unifies experience and representation. These assemblies of forms and formats, and their proliferate associations and allusions, provide ways into *The Labyrinth of Rooms: An Architectural Allegory*; the question left for the reader is how (and what) to get out...

John McMorrough
Ann Arbor, Summer 2023

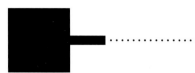

HOPE

Human woke up in a square room with blind walls.
Confused, they looked around, left and right, and
       blinked many times.
Human did not know where they were or how they
       got there.
They asked themselves, even without knowing who
       they themselves were: Is this an
       underground room, or is it inside a
       spaceship gliding across the galaxy?
Human could not find an answer to this question.
Then, Human looked behind them and noticed
       a corridor, which felt like a sign of hope.
Human entered the corridor promptly, without fear,
       without hesitation, only with eagerness.

PULLED

The corridor led Human to another room.

This room was rectangular, and it had another corridor
leading out.

But Human did not enter this corridor promptly.

They stopped to think, and asked themselves another
question: Should I go through this corridor
and perhaps reach a new room with a new
shape, or should I stay here, or even go
back to the square?

Again, Human could not find an answer to their
question, their mind still disoriented by
the strange surroundings.

And yet, even without a good reason to do so, they
started walking forward, as if pulled by
an invisible rope, as if called by a siren
at the corridor's end, as if a mystical
magnetism were having its magical way.

ADVENTURE

Human found the shape of the next room difficult
to describe.
They thought of word after word, one phrase then
another, but none seemed to match the
shape perfectly.
This did not make Human sad; it actually made
them happy.
Human wondered whether these rooms were like
little puzzles, little games they could
endlessly play.
This possibility excited Human very much, and they
imagined the wonderful adventures they
could have: walking and discovering
and analyzing, comparing shapes, sizes,
and numbers.
What fun this could be!
And with such optimism, Human walked on.

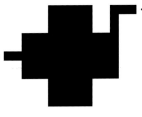

WISDOM

The fourth room had four alcoves, and each had
        a message for Human.
The first alcove said: Each room is a Universe, and
        the Universe is a room.
The second alcove said: You have infinite choices,
        but only one path is possible.
The third alcove said: Everything is different, yet
        everything is similar.
The fourth alcove said: Remember this, meaning is
        only as you mean it.
Human was overwhelmed by the wisdom of these
        messages, and found in them an infinite
        capacity for solace.
Grateful and humbled, Human bowed to the room
        four times in four directions.
Then Human walked out the corridor.

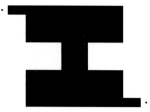

QUESTIONS

Even after some serious thought, Human could
not reach a satisfying understanding
of the room.
Then, they considered a possibility: perhaps these
rooms are beyond answers and truth;
perhaps they are machines for asking
beautiful questions.
But, if so, who operates those machines?
Human wondered whether they could be such an
operator, one clever and courageous
enough to ask a beautiful question.
Certainly, that would require a great deal of intellectual
skill, and much experience with unraveling
geometric knots.
Being humble, Human was aware they did not have
such expertise; but being audacious,
Human hoped that one day they would.

ETIQUETTE

Human reached a triangular room.
Though tempted, Human did not walk along its
        hypotenuse.
Human was too polite for that, and though yet a
        beginner, they were still versed enough
        in the etiquette of shapes to avoid such a
        transgression.
Human walked along the two other sides of the triangle,
        pausing at the right angle—that most
        perfect point—to make an oath:
        In this room and every other,
          From this day until forever,
         Grand, glorious geometry,
            I am yours,
            Human.

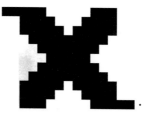

EYES

Human touched every wall.
Human felt every corner.
Human studied the room from every angle, noting
        how the slightest change in perspective
        also changed its character.
Human hopped like a rabbit, crouched like a cat, and
        crawled like a snake, constantly changing
        the eyes with which they looked at the
        room: to glance then glare, to squint
        then stare.
This intensity of looking was Human's technique to
        intimidate the room, force it to make
        an error, and gradually let slip its secrets.
By the time Human was satisfied, their knowledge
        of the room's geometry was intimate,
        magnificent, all but total.
They took the corridor to the next room as someone
        departing their lifelong home: dislodged.

BAD

The room was square in shape, but circuitous
       in personality.
Round and round the square, Human walked and
       walked, always ending where they started,
       but with less than what they had.
Eventually, Human became tired and bored and a
       little bit angry.
Realizing that all their efforts in this room had been
       futile, Human started to shout: This room
       is not nice, and I do not like it, and it
       is very bad, and it is the worst room, and
       I will leave immediately!
As they walked to the corridor, Human's voice traveled
       round and round the square, slapping
       them with every lap, and making Human
       hate the room even more.

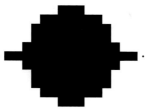

ECSTASY

Perfection!
Beauty of beauties!
A wonder to behold!
Human stood in the center of the circular room,
        spinning like a tranced dancer,
        overwhelmed and overjoyed.
Human's emotions spilled and splashed around the
        room, torquing into a dizzying whirlpool
        that sent them to the extreme heights
        of ecstasy.
Having been swept far beyond the limits of their
        body and mind, Human collapsed with
        exhaustion.
When Human woke up, they ran out the room,
        laughing, terrified.

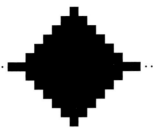

BEYOND

Everything was calm at first, then Human was
                ambushed by a swarm of stinging
                questions:
If I am inside this room, then what is this room inside of?
If these walls are keeping me in, then what are they
                keeping out?
If beyond these rooms is space, is it shaped or is it
                shapeless?
If beyond these rooms is void, is it new or was it always?
If beyond these rooms is possible, will I reach it?
If beyond these rooms exists, are there Humans?
Human thought once and twice and more, but could
                not answer and could not quit.

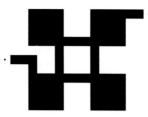

DOUBT

In this room, numbers and geometry were not in
        alignment, an absolute rarity in this corner
        of the Universe.
Numbers said one, while geometry said four, and no
        amount of counting or measuring allowed
        Human to bring one up to four or four
        down to one.
Human knew that one and four were not the same.
One and four are not the same, Human mumbled with
        a hint of doubt.
But what if one and four are the same?
I am one Human, so am I also four Humans?
And suddenly, Human saw their body explode into
        a hundred million particles that shot away
        and became one with the walls and the
        rooms and the corridors, one with the
        Labyrinth itself.

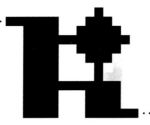

BEST

What makes a room better than other rooms?
Is the biggest room the best? Or is it the one with the
               purest geometry? Or is it the hardest room
               to make?
And what does better even mean, and for whom?
Should the room be better for Human to occupy?
               Or better as a neighbor to other rooms?
               Or should it simply be better for itself,
               a geometric excellence for its own sake?
Human walked from room to room, rambling like
               a mad architect:
    I cannot choose, I cannot choose, I cannot choose
               The best of rooms.
       I cannot say, I cannot say, I cannot say
               In which I'd stay.

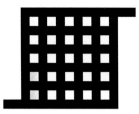

TREASURE

Far from being a fool, Human immediately realized that
this room was a double-faced trickster.
But Human was not about to be bamboozled, oh no.
They knew the room was pretending to be the same
thing, just repeated many times.
The room wanted Human to quickly pass through,
as if there was nothing special to see, as
if it was hiding no precious secrets.
But Human was smarter than that, oh yes.
Human spent long and equal time in every spot and
every corner, patiently searching for
geometric treasure.
And eventually, as expected, Human caught the sparkle
of gold.

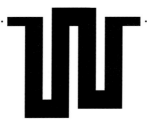

BLUR

Human imagined walking through the intestines of
        a gigantic snake.
Human turned right, left, left, right, right, left, left, right,
        hoping for something to change, but the
        space remained narrow and long.
Exasperated, Human asked: If this is a room, then why
        does it feel like a corridor?
Previously, Human thought that rooms were not
        corridors, and corridors were not rooms,
        and that it was easy to tell one from
        the other.
But now, this did not seem easy at all.
The room was hard to define, like a blurry edge between
        two shapes.
Where did one end and the other begin?
Or, perhaps, Human nervously whispered, there are no
        edges at all.

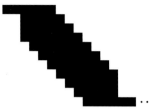

KNOWLEDGE

In a moment of epiphany, Human realized that senses
do not sense everything.
Human perceived some aspects of these rooms, but
infinitely more remained imperceptible.
And no matter how hard they looked and thought,
entire dimensions of space remained
invisible for Human, unseeable by the
eye and unimaginable by the mind.
Human was defeated by this realization, for what was
the point of pursuing knowledge if most
of that knowledge was beyond reach?
Human felt like a tiny diver trying to map an endless
ocean.
Suddenly, the mind-boggling fullness of reality seemed
uncanny, a crushing burden marked only
by its absence.
There is just so much out there, Human managed
to say, so much and so much more
than that.

FEELING

The room was divided into four quarters.
The quarters were perfect squares, exactly the
        same size, yet each gave Human
        a different feeling.
Those feelings were sudden, rising and fading within
        moments of Human entering each quarter,
        but they were also intense and vivid and
        tough to forget.
The first quarter felt like it should be filled with soil
        and planted with white and blue flowers.
The second felt like a prison cell—cold and barren
        and forcing introspection.
The third felt suitable for proposing to one's partner,
        and then years later agreeing on an
        amicable divorce in the same spot.
The fourth felt familiar, as if Human had been there
        as a child, and that, for Human, was the
        most disturbing feeling.

COERCION

Human swallowed their pride and did as the room
     demanded.
There was no other way if Human was to continue
     this adventure.
Human is smart and strong, and undoubtedly a
     formidable opponent even to the most
     coercive of rooms, but still, Human
     cannot overcome a room exerting all its
     geometric force towards a single diagram.
Such single-minded architecture cannot be defeated;
     it must be negotiated with or submitted to.
Human accepted this and did what was necessary,
     for only a fool storms a castle without
     an army.

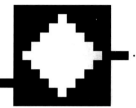

MEANING

Human quickly decided upon the room's geometry:
          four right triangles connected to form
          a square.
Then Human reconsidered: it is a square from which
          a smaller square, turned forty-five degrees,
          has been subtracted.
Had they continued this exercise, more plausible
          descriptions of the room would
          have emerged.
But Human did not continue, for such an exercise
          felt pointless.
Human complained: All these shapes, doing their little
          tricks, acting profound, as if they had
          something to say, while desperate to
          hide the truth; they are all meaningless,
          every single one of them.
Human was tired and did not want to play this
          game anymore.
With drooping spirits, they walked out of the room.

PLOT

Human started to suspect that corridors were not
        so innocent.
They feigned neutrality, pretending to serve but
        a practical purpose, but what if they had
        a secret agenda?
For example, why do some open into a room's long
        side while others open into its short side?
And why do some break the middle of a wall while
        others enter through a corner?
And why do some cooperate in a shared plan while
        others act as private agents?
This cannot all be a coincidence; it makes no
        functional sense!
They must be plotting something, those sneaky
        little corridors; Human was sure of it.

SEQUENCE

Human walked into a rectangular room, then took
a short corridor to a triangular room.
Human walked out the corridor of the triangular
room, turned around halfway in, and
walked back.
Human reentered the triangular room, then took the
short corridor to the rectangular room.
The same two rooms, their order switched, made
all the difference to Human.
The experience of the mind, the feeling of the heart,
and the imprint on the soul that the
two rooms left on Human one way,
were entirely different the other way.
Human realized that they were not only visiting
a number of rooms, but rooms in
a designed sequence.

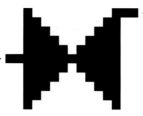

SPACE

Between the two selfsame rooms, mirror images of
       each other, there was a tiny passageway,
       barely wide enough for Human to
       traverse, and in that tiny passageway
       Human collapsed into a knot of limbs,
       neck straining to shove head towards
       navel, eyes tightly shut, tense arms
       wrapping around chest-embracing knees,
       skin boiling and skin freezing, veins
       pulsing and veins clenching, Human
       shook and shivered, having suddenly been
       stricken by a fear of open space.
Space: that most totalitarian dimension of existence.

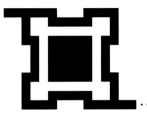

ITCH

Human's by now extra-developed sense of space was
on fire.
Human desperately ran through the jagged corridor,
lapping its circuit again and again, looking
for the hidden space whose presence felt
so real that Human could almost touch,
but could not touch.
There was something there, something more,
something implied and believed but
impossible to prove.
This room afflicted Human with a phantom itch that
could not be scratched; satisfaction
was prohibited.
This is an architecture of rejection, Human moaned,
an architecture of prohibition:
I love it, it loves me not...
I love it, it loves me not...
I love it, it loves me not...

BLESSING

Delicate, lacelike openings tenderly split and sewed
themselves back together in an intricate
pattern of solids and space.
A dazzling geometric dance frozen a second before its
ultimate emotional explosion.
Purified beauty, beauty itself, and nothing but beauty.
Tears of awe rolled down Human's face as they slowly
walked around the room, placing their feet
as gently as a devout worshiper entering
a crystal temple.
What a blessing, Human thought, what a blessing for
me to be here, now, experiencing this.
And in that moment Human was more certain than ever
that this journey was worth more than
can be humanly repaid.

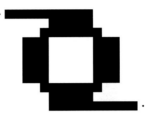

TRUTH

The room was precise, apportioned perfectly, and
         Human was impressed.
A harmonic system regulated every measurable
         dimension in the room with every other.
By studying any small part of the room, Human was
         able to discern the logic of the whole;
         and from understanding the whole,
         Human could deduce the meaning of
         every tiny part.
The closer Human looked, the more truths they found—
         endless truths—so much so that Human
         wondered whether the reality of the entire
         Universe was piece by piece embedded
         in the architecture of this room, an
         architecture of absolute mathematics.

OPTIONS

Human walked to the end of a thin rectangular space,
     and was there presented with two options.
The corridor going straight ahead clearly led to the
     next room.
The corridor to Human's left clearly led to the rest
     of this room, probably terminating in
     a dead-end.
This was clear to Human because the shapes of these
     rooms were not random: there was a
     common geometric sensibility governing
     the design of the Labyrinth, and Human
     had begun to grasp it.
Instinctively, Human turned left, wanting to see what
     else the room had to offer, but then
     stopped a few steps into the corridor,
     and asked: Do I really want to see the
     end of this corridor?
I do not, Human confidently answered, then turned
     back and walked to the next room.

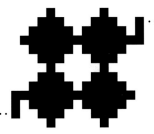

WHY

Human asked the Diamonds Rooms: What do you want from me?

The Diamonds Room answered: I want nothing from you, Human.

Human: Do you not want me to study your geometry and admire your shape?

Diamonds Room: No, I do not want that, Human.

Human: Then why are you so geometrically elegant and shapely to my eyes?

Diamonds Room: I am how I am, for myself, before you even had eyes, Human.

Human: But my eyes respond to the way you are. Why?

Diamonds Room: That is for you to answer, Human.

Human: I do not understand.

Diamonds Room: Because you are Human, you never will.

ANSWERS

Upon entering the room, Human started thinking out
                loud, like a young and confident professor
                searching for answers they are sure will
                soon be coming:
A circle is perfect, that much is obvious.
This room is half a circle, but it is not perfection halved.
This semicircle has a fullness to it, a sense
                of completeness, the calmness of
                something entire.
So how is that possible?
If geometry cannot halve all the answers, then it must
                not have all the answers.
And truth must lie elsewhere.
And lie it certainly does.
And with that dramatic line, the professor left the room.

INFINITE

Human walked into a large rectangular space and
        thought about the infinite vastness of
        the Universe.
Then Human walked into a smaller rectangular space
        and thought about the earth and the sky,
        and a series of connected walls, and
        a series of connected rooms.
Finally, Human walked into the smallest rectangular
        space, and their thoughts shrunk down
        to the scale of atoms, then down to
        the particles that make up atoms, then
        down to the impossible spaces between
        particles, and then everything went black
        and blank and nothingness filled that
        infinite vastness of the Universe.

CHANGE

Human found no room.

The corridor just kept going and going, occasionally turning, but mostly going straight.

The familiar rhythm of rooms and corridors that structured Human's life since they awoke in that square room was suddenly shattered.

If even such an unthinkable happening is possible, Human wondered, what other rules of the Universe are similarly subject to sudden and arbitrary change?

If monumental change is as simple as this, Human asked, then what is separating my ordered life from total chaos?

But also, Human dared to think, what if the next big change is one that I design?

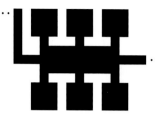

DECISION

The room felt like a potential home.

Human imagined how they would use each of its
spaces if they settled here.

One space for standing, one for sitting, one for
sleeping, one for playing, one for thinking,
one for singing.

What a lovely and orderly life that would be!

Human knew that all they had to do for this life to
become a reality was to make a decision,
a decision not to walk through that
corridor to the next room, a decision to
give up the adventure and accept a less
exciting life, a decision to be content with
a good present and stop searching for
a better future, a decision that Human
was desperate to make, but couldn't.

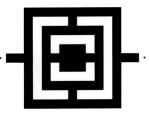

BORING

The room was perfectly symmetrical.
Its proportions were exquisite and its geometry sublime.
Solids and voids were impeccably balanced.
The journey from periphery to center was ingeniously
        choreographed.
Not an opening was out of place, and not a thing
        could be improved.
Every texture on every surface, every glittering beam
        of light, they dazzled the eye and enticed
        the mind.
In short, the room was a transcendent work of art.
If only it were not so boring and soulless, Human
        grumbled, it would have been a pretty
        good room.

MIDDLE

Human imagined the room used to be long and
             straight, before a giant grabbed it and
             bent it in half.
Human stood where the two halves met and
             contemplated things in halves, things
             with two sides, two-faced things, binary
             things, things at once single and double,
             things always made in pairs, things
             that need an equal other, things whose
             middles are always marked, and so on.
Then Human wondered whether they had reached the
             halfway point of their adventure, or if this
             was just the beginning, or if they were
             only a few steps away from the very,
             very end?

MOOD

There were too many little corridors for Human to
count, and honestly, even had there been
fewer corridors, Human would not have
counted them.
That is because of the mood Human was in, which was
not a counting mood, but a brooding mood.
Human was brooding and brooding, over this and over
that and over every other silly something.
What Human did not know was that had they found the
will to start counting the room's corridors,
walls, corners, or any other geometric
feature, their brooding mood would have
slowly subsided, for the precision of
counting and the haziness of brooding
cannot coexist.
Unaware of this, Human brooded on.

HYSTERIA

Human quickly identified the room as U-shaped.
Then Human thought of a funny joke, and laughed
        aloud: U-shaped or You-shaped?
Shaking with giggles, Human tried to imagine a You-
        shaped room.
Every new image they thought of amused them more
        than the last.
Then Human thought of an even funnier joke, and they
        laughed even louder, with tears of joy
        streaming down their cheeks.
They blurted out: You-shaped room or Me-shaped room?
Human started howling with laughter, rolling on the
        floor, slapping themselves uncontrollably,
        almost hysterical, their cackles echoing
        from room to room.

TIME

Some rooms were built through toil and trouble, brick
         by brick, with tired hands and tired souls.
This room just one day sprouted, unexpected and
         uninvited, without an effort or a worry, like
         a flower in a garden.
Some rooms will weather over time, chafing and
         cracking and losing their shine, destined
         to fall apart and disappear, as if they never
         were there.
This room was in perpetual bloom, always in high spring
         and higher spirits, always supple and
         strong and getting stronger still, always in
         the mindless glory of youth

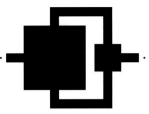

FORGETTING

Human reached the middle of a square, and lingered
there.
Then Human took a corridor to another square, which
was smaller, but Human was not sure
by how much.
So Human took the corridor back to the bigger square
to study its size, only to realize that they
had already forgotten the size of the
smaller square.
Human then took the corridor back to the smaller
square to remember its size.
Just like that, again and again, Human went from bigger
to smaller square and back, unable to
grasp the size of the one before forgetting
the size of the other.
Human was stuck, caught in the ebb and flow of amnesia.

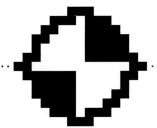

TERROR

Human was convinced that if this room could speak, it
would say to them: Leave, now, or else...
The room had corners as sharp as steel blades, walls
like shattered mirrors, floors like beds of
nails, and ceilings threatening death from
above, like a guillotine.
Whether the room posed an actual threat to Human's
body was doubtful, but they still felt jittery,
taking apprehensive steps, looking back
often, afraid to turn corners, unnerved by
the sound of their own racing heart.
Nevertheless, Human took a principled stance, refusing
to leave, not wanting to submit to the
room's aggressive posture: I will not
negotiate with this architecture of terror.
But that only lasted so long, their growing anxiety—like
a corrosive acid—eventually dissolved
their resolve.
Human, clumsy with fear, ran for the exit.

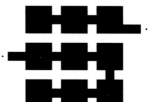

EDGE

It was not the nine squares that fascinated Human,
    but the small thresholds that connected
    them, those little in-betweens that joined
    one square to another.
Perhaps those thresholds, Human pondered, are
    sovereign sites in themselves.
Contrary to what Human assumed, the middles of
    the squares were the least interesting
    areas in the room, for in those middles
    nothing happened.
Instead, all the action, all the movement, all the magic
    of architecture happened as Human
    passed through the portals that led from
    one space to another.
Human realized that the nature of the center was
    always defined at the edge.

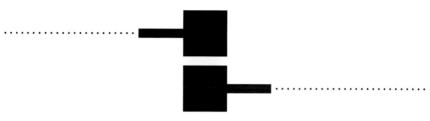

SNAP

For a panicky moment that seemed to last forever,
        Human thought that they had reached
        the end of their journey, for they found
        themselves in a square room with no
        exit other than the corridor from which
        they had come.
But just as that panic was about to turn into fiery
        anger, debilitating terror, or utter anguish,
        Human inexplicably snapped out of
        existence, remained nonexistent for
        a blissful wink of time, and then snapped
        back into existence.
Human was still in a square room with one corridor
        leading out of it, but neither room
        nor corridor was the same, and the
        path to their journey's continuation was
        again open.

BRIDGE

Human conceived of the room's corridors as
                    outstretched limbs, reaching for what
                    space always desires: union.
Only one corridor managed to bridge the two sides of
                    the room, while the other four ended in
                    disappointment.
Human entered each of the failed corridors, gently
                    caressed the seams of their cold walls,
                    whispered tender words of friendship,
                    and paused in secret spots to make
                    little prayers.
Human told the corridors that for Human, they were
                    not failures at all, but noble martyrs in the
                    eternal struggle between falling together
                    and falling apart.
Sometimes, two banks are left unbridged.

QUIET

Human's head brimmed with things to say about the
          room; it was like a great bubbling cauldron
          of hearty ideas.
They could have said nice things, perhaps about the
          room's tight form and articulated skin.
They could have said mean things, perhaps about it
          being both too fussy and too boring,
          both too much and too little.
They could have asked deep questions, perhaps about
          the room's visual meaning, emotional
          state, or ideological basis.
They could have pontificated endlessly about its spatial
          qualities, geometric definition, and
          architectural soul.
They could have said any of those things or others like
          them, had they chosen to, but instead
          they breathed—deeply—and stayed quiet.

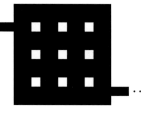

POWER

Human felt four times bigger, three times stronger, and
       twice the Human they were before walking
       into this room.
In a room like this—built solid like a mountain,
       buttressed by nine mighty columns, and
       wrapped by four massive walls—who
       would not feel like they could take over
       the world?
Eyes red and crazed, blood pulsing with venom, Human
       barked at the mute walls, punched every
       side of every column, desperate to
       establish dominance over this architecture
       of power.
But not long after, tired and bruised, Human lay down,
       mumbled "I am Sovereign" again and
       again, until the Sovereign passed out.

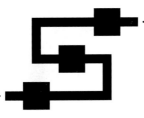

PATTERN

Human considered how they reacted to different kinds
of spaces, and became uneasy when they
noticed their own predictability.
When the space was narrow and long, like a corridor,
Human walked quickly, rarely stopping
to look around.
But when the space opened up and took the form of
a distinct geometry, like a square or a circle,
Human always stopped to study it.
The more Human dwelled on this pattern, the more
it disturbed them, for it suggested that
their actions were determined by the
architecture around them.
Was Human free to make their choices, or were
they nothing more than a marionette
whose every action and thought was
predetermined by the one who designed
this Labyrinth?

VOICE

And in that fateful moment, the room violently shook,
     and a Gargantuan Voice boomed like
     mighty thunder:
OH HUMAN, CHILD OF HUMANS, WHAT HAVE YOU
     GAINED FROM THESE ROOMS?
Human: Nothing that I can hold, nothing that you can see.
Gargantuan Voice: AND WHAT HAVE YOU SPENT IN THE
     NAME OF THESE ROOMS?
Human: Everything, all my time, all my energy, all my
     thoughts.
Gargantuan Voice: SO WHY DO YOU KEEP DOING WHAT
     HAS TAKEN EVERYTHING FROM YOU, AND
     GIVEN NOTHING IN RETURN?
Human: Because I am Human, I must continue until
     the end.
And the Gargantuan Voice was silent for a moment,
     then exploded in laughter—long, crashing
     waves of laughter that left Human
     trembling with perturbation.

CLARITY

Human approached the three-mouthed room.

Each mouth had something to tell Human.

The first mouth said: Enter.

The second mouth said: Look.

The third mouth said: Leave.

Without a word, Human complied with the three orders
of the three mouths.

The orders were simple, and Human was able to perform
them efficiently.

Human wondered how their experience would be
different if all rooms were as direct about
their purpose as the three-mouthed room.

Would that have made this adventure more enjoyable,
or would such clarity of purpose have
made it not an adventure at all?

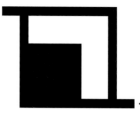

THIRTEEN

Human did thirteen things in the room, with the room,
and for the room:

1. Walked in.
2. Chose between two directions.
3. Pressed their body into a concave corner.
4. Slid their palm down a convex corner.
5. Knocked on walls and analyzed the sound.
6. Emitted short yelps and listened for an echo.
7. Measured lengths in number of footsteps.
8. Measured heights in number of upright Humans.
9. Walked the corridor with closed eyes.
10. Walked the corridor backwards.
11. Imagined a horizontal section of the room.
12. Imagined a vertical section of the room.
13. Walked out.

DESIGNER

Human found that in the repetitive architecture of long
               corridors, their mind was clearest and
               most prone to ask big questions.
This time, Human was considering the origin of this
               Labyrinth and their own existence within it.
Every right angle, every intelligent layout, every sign of
               intentionality proved to Human that this
               Labyrinth had a First Designer.
But what mad and powerful force could think up such
               an unlikely place, and then have the
               craftiness to build it?
And of all the existing beings in the Universe, and the
               ones that before existed, and those that
               will one day exist, why am I the Human
               who ended up here?

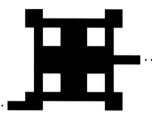

ACTING

The room had a refined geometry, elegant and grand,
        like the court of a well-loved monarch.
Human closed their eyes to imagine scenes in that royal
        court, then opened their eyes to decide
        where each character would stand and
        how each action would unfold.
The monarch sits on a throne over there. Next to her
        is the wise vizier, and flanking them are
        unsmiling guards clutching sheathed
        swords. In front of them is a jester
        swallowing a knife, or a wretched soul
        hearing a verdict upon their life;
        and all around are the people—cheering
        or jeering—riveted by the spectacle.
Human spent hours acting out each part.

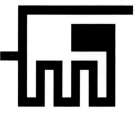

SURPRISE

The room offered a twisting corridor, somewhat
          tedious, but at its end Human found
          a worthwhile surprise.
Human's brain raced to find appropriate analogies for
          this two-step game the room just played:
Architecture, like a bow, is about the draw and the
          release; like boxing, it is about the feint
          and the punch; like a drama, it is about the
          cliffhanger before the finale; like hiking,
          it is about the ascent then the view; like
          a joke, it is setup then punchline; like
          a new year, it is countdown then fireworks;
          like a magic trick, it is disappearance then
          reappearance; like an intervention, it is
          the lie then the truth; like Ramadan,
          it is fasting then feasting; like learning,
          it is arrogance then modesty; like creation,
          it is nothing then something, darkness
          then light.

CHAOS

Human walked into an inexplicable room, a room
impossible to understand, doomed to be
an everlasting enigma.
That was not because the room was hiding its
architectural logic too well, but because
there was no logic at all.
And it was not that the room had once had a sense of
order that was subsequently lost, nor was
it that Human had somehow missed a
geometric clue which, if recovered, would
render the composition intelligible.
No, no, it was much worse than that.
The chaos of the room was not caused, it did not
happen; the chaos there was originary,
of the same primal stuff from which the
Universe was born.
There, Human faced a pure and ancient chaos taking
the guise of space: anarchy reified.

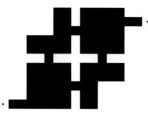

PURPOSE

Human was at first pleased with the geometry of the
               room: the way it balanced division and
               connection, difference and repetition,
               parts and wholes.
The room had the air of expertise casually shown off:
               no fuss, no drama, just good design.
But as Human started walking to the next room, having
               been fully satisfied with this one, they
               were stopped by some uncomfortable
               thoughts:
Yes, the room is undoubtedly a wonderful creation,
               but is that enough?
Where is its beating heart, its faith and conviction,
               its sublime purpose, its passionate case
               for the need to exist?

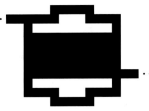

ALIVE

As soon as Human entered the rectangular room, they felt waves of emotion washing over them, seeming to emanate from an invisible source at its center.

The closer Human walked to the center, the more intense the emotional field became, eventually feeling like explosive pulses bursting from Human's core, quickly overwhelming them, risking injury, and forcing Human's retreat to an adjacent corridor.

But Human kept returning to the rectangle's center, for the emotional intensity they felt there was intoxicating: beyond pleasure and pain, beyond good and evil, it was a pure density of sensation that for the very first time convinced Human that they were fully and unquestionably alive.

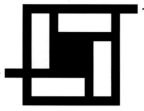

RITUAL

Human imagined four priests in the middle of the
square, holding hands, spinning around,
and chanting in unison.
Their voices gradually rose, building to a frightening
crescendo, until they were screaming
nothing but beastly sounds, their
synchronized ritual crumbling into total
disharmony.
When things could not get uglier, suddenly the priests
let go of each other's hands, ran out of
the square through separate corridors,
traveled clockwise around the outer
perimeter, and each used a separate
corridor to walk back and reassemble in
the middle.
They took a moment to calm their breathing, then
found each other's hands, and restarted
their chanting in barely audible whispers.
Human could not explain what made them imagine
such a scene.

BIRTH

The room was comprised of two triangular spaces,
        connected by an umbilical cord, as if one
        side of the room were providing the other
        with sustenance, cultivating its geometry.
This mental image that Human started to play with—of
        architecture feeding architecture and
        space nourishing space—led Human to
        consider a fascinating possibility:
What if this Labyrinth was not finished?
What if it was still gestating, still taking shape, slowly
        growing in size and definition, its end
        stretching away from Human even as
        Human walked towards it?
What if the end of this journey was not an exit, but a
        birth, expected to happen the moment
        Human's maturation was complete?

INDIFFERENT

It had been a while since Human had entered a simple
      room like this one.
Lately, the rooms had favored complexity to a fault:
      pompously designed, obsessively
      articulated, desperate to be special,
      craving attention and approval.
To the contrary, this room was indifferent to Human's
      opinions, who found this indifference
      comforting, allowing them to rest their
      critical faculties, and for a moment exist
      thoughtlessly.
There was no need for judgment in this room,
      nor for proving one's cleverness, nor for
      applause, nor a reaction of any sort;
      nothing was needed.
Things were the way they were, and that was all.

MALLEABILITY

As Human walked around the two squares, one bigger
than the other, they started thinking about
the malleability of space.

It was hard at first, since the two squares looked so
permanent, as did every wall in the
Labyrinth, but Human persisted and
eventually succeeded in making their
mind see what their eyes could not.

With their imagination ignited, Human saw a great
carnival of shape-shifting rooms:
expanding and shrinking, separating and
joining, bending and twisting.

Human realized that shapes were in fact alive, always
transforming, always in transition, and that
the well-crafted operation can turn any
shape into any other.

GUT

This room was not about what the eye can see, nor
        what the hand can touch, nor what the
        ear can hear, nor even what the mind
        can discern.
This room was all about the gut, and Human's gut was
        turning sour.
It was not so much a feeling of danger, but of moral
        corruption, as if the architectural
        substance of the room had degenerated,
        its spatial character reeking like
        a decomposing carcass.
What it became was more cynical than sinister,
        an architecture so trapped in its own
        insecurity and pessimism that it inspired
        nothing but a profound sense of pity.

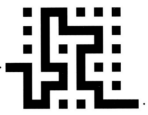

IRREFUTABLE

If some corridors in this Labyrinth seemed to chart
arbitrary paths, turning for no reason,
branching without explanation, and
feeling as purposeless as a rambling
acquaintance stumbling through a
pointless story in search of a satisfying
ending that never comes, this corridor
was different.

Though it was not clear why it took the path it did,
Human felt there was an irrefutable
argument for every segment of its
composition; every decision in its
making seemed serious, deliberate, and
impossible to improve.

It felt as if had this corridor's path been any different, no
matter how slight the change, the results
would have been of a cataclysmic nature,
world-ending; or perhaps there would not
have even been a world to end.

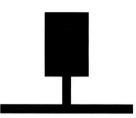

RESPECT

Unlike every other room, this one was merely optional. Human could ignore it and keep walking to whatever was next.

This architecture was not forced; it was presented to Human as a possibility, an offering subject to their decision to accept it.

Human understood this as a gesture of respect, shown by the Labyrinth of rooms to the one who walked it.

It was an acknowledgment that though Human did not choose to have this adventure, they could still make decisions to shape its unfolding.

Perhaps even, it was a slight apology, owed to the Human who—despite everything—walked this Labyrinth in earnest, and took its indignities in stride.

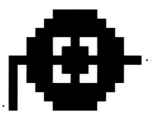

BEAUTY

Human saw a room abundant with beauty, but was
        wise enough to know that most of that
        beauty sprang from their own eyes.
It was as if the room were singing a lovely melody,
        but it was Human who had written its
        rhyming words.
A beautiful mind sees beautiful things, and in every
        sincere architecture it sees a reason for
        celebration and gratitude.
Human did not always have a beautiful mind, certainly
        not at the start of this journey, but now
        they did.
All those rooms—visited, studied, and felt—had left their
        mark on Human's mind, had sharpened its
        faculties, yes, but had also softened it to
        the wonders of life.

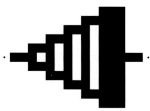

DELIVERANCE

The room was organized as a series of thin spaces,
        like layers of fabric folded upon each
        other, gradually growing in length,
        and finally opening into a spacious
        rectangle.
After the constriction of the thin spaces, the rectangle
        was a relief, both to body and soul: it was
        large enough for Human to breathe
        a healthy lungful of air.
Every stress must end in release, Human thought, and
        every hardship must lead to deliverance:
        that is the way of the world.
All that was needed to reach that necessary paradise
        was ceaseless movement, a belief that
        it really exists, an interest in seeking its
        palmy paths, and the willingness to ever
        walk to the next room.

CYCLE

As soon as Human entered the room, they were
                alarmed by a feeling of familiarity and
                a sudden flood of emotions rushing from
                the distant past.
Human realized that this square room was the exact
                shape and size as the room they woke up
                in the day this journey started.
The two square architectures were identical, but the
                experience was not the same.
The explanation was clear: the Labyrinth was a cycle,
                but not a perfect one, for though the
                walls were the walls, Human was a Human
                transformed.
And since Human was not the same, neither was the
                square they saw.

FORWARD

Beginnings can be endings, and endings beginnings,
        just like in this Labyrinth: you cannot leave
        one room without entering another.
As had happened many times before, Human was
        confronted by a corridor leading to an
        unknown place.
And though Human had significantly changed—made
        impressive strides, had gained experience
        and wisdom—they were in some ways
        much the same as they had always been:
        thrust forward by two pairs of wandering
        legs and wondering eyes.
Human entered the corridor promptly, without fear,
        without hesitation, only with eagerness.

AFTERWORD

There is the space inside my skull and the space outside my skin.

I can call them *mental space* and *physical space*.

And despite seeming unrelated—one psycho-logical and the other material—the flow between them appears almost seamless: thoughts becoming things and things becoming thoughts.

For example, I stand inside a room, I see its walls clearly, and when I close my eyes, I see that same room inside my mind, just as clearly, though in a different way.

The Labyrinth of Rooms is a story about how the shape of architecture can change the way we think, and how the shape of our thoughts can change the way we see architecture. Stated otherwise, the story conceives of the human life as a series of settings that stage the coevolution of mental space and physical space.

Human, the story's protagonist, can be any one of us, and their journey from the first room to the last room is the journey of a lifetime: it has its ups and downs, moments of clarity and moments of confusion, but overall it bends towards greater knowledge and wisdom.

What I hope for most is that you enjoy the story and find in its words and images the same pleasure I found when putting them together.

Ali AlYousefi
Kuwait City, Spring 2023

EDITIONS

Publishers of Architecture, Art, and Design
Gordon Goff: Publisher

www.oroeditions.com
info@oroeditions.com

Published by ORO Editions

Graphic Design: Sharaf Studio
Text: Ali AlYousefi
ORO Managing Editor: Kirby Anderson

10 9 8 7 6 5 4 3 2 1 First Edition
Library of Congress data available upon request.
World Rights: Available

ISBN: 978-1-957183-72-5

Color Separations and Printing:
ORO Editions, Inc.
Printed in China.

International Distribution:
www.oroeditions.com/distribution

ORO Editions makes a continuous effort to minimize the overall carbon footprint of its publications. As part of this goal, ORO Editions, in association with Global ReLeaf, arranges to plant trees to replace those used in the manufacturing of the paper produced for its books. Global ReLeaf is an international campaign run by American Forests, one of the world's oldest nonprofit conservation organizations. Global ReLeaf is American Forests' education and action program that helps individuals, organizations, agencies, and corporations improve the local and global environment by planting and caring for trees.